RED DAWN
A WINDS OF WAR NOVELLA

William C. Dietz

PHOENIX PICK

ARC MANOR
ROCKVILLE, MARYLAND

✳

SHAHID MAHMUD
PUBLISHER

www.ArcManor.com

Cover art by Dany V.

Other Books by William C. Dietz

THE WINDS OF WAR SERIES
Red Ice
Red Flood
Red Dragon
Red Thunder
Red Tide
Red Sands
Red River
Red Dog
Red Line

AMERICA RISING SERIES
Into the Guns
Seek and Destroy
Battle Hymn

MUTANT FILES SERIES
Deadeye
Redzone
Graveyard

LEGION OF THE DAMNED SERIES
Legion of the Damned
The Final Battle
By Blood Alone
By Force of Arms
For More Than Glory
For Those Who Fell
When All Seems Lost
When Duty Calls
A Fighting Chance
Andromeda's Fall
Andromeda's Choice
Andromeda's War

ISBN: 978-1-64973-183-8
First Edition September 2025

An imprint of Arc Manor Inc.
www.ArcManor.com

This novella is dedicated to Marjorie,
the through line in my life, and my other half.

❦

PREFACE

AS *Red Dawn* begins, a global battle is underway. After attacking and sinking the Destroyer *USS Stacy Heath*, the Chinese invaded Tibet and India counterattacked. In response to the attack on the destroyer, and in an effort to support India, the U.S. sent 20,000 soldiers and Marines to join the fight.

Meanwhile, Russian President Toplin saw the conflict as an opportunity to invade Ukraine, which left NATO with no choice but to respond.

Eventually, in an attempt to capitalize on the worldwide chaos, North Korea invaded the south and captured Seoul. That forced the U.S., and its ally Japan, to try and dislodge the northerners—even as Russia and China brought their forces to bear.

And now, as the war continues, no one is safe.

CHAPTER ONE

Benito Juarez International Airport, Mexico

THE sun was low in the sky, and the thunder created by a departing passenger plane made it difficult to hear, as Vice President Al Hayden and a coterie of Mexican officials gathered near Air Force Two.

The men shook hands, and women kissed cheeks, while Secret Service agents stood with their backs turned to the Vice President and their hands in the ready position. They knew, as everyone did, that WWIII was being fought everywhere. Airports included.

Hayden accepted one last kiss and said, "*Adios,*" to the Mexican Secretary of Foreign Affairs, before making his way to the roll-up stairs that led up and into Air Force Two.

The forward section of the plane included a communications center, galley, lavatory and 10 business class seats. That's where Hayden and his senior staff members sat, while junior functionaries, Secret Service agents, and members of the traveling press were seated aft.

Once the passengers were settled in, the plane's copilot, Captain T.L. Jones, made the usual announcements, and a crewmember delivered drinks. A bourbon for Hayden, and a screwdriver for his Chief of Staff, Emory Vale. "So," Vale said. "What do you think? How did it go?"

Hayen took a sip. "President Ramos is a slippery bastard. That's what it takes to lead a neutral country. But, given the amount of freight that flows through the Panama Canal, the big ditch is important to him—just as it should be.

"So, Ramos promised to call Loban, and pressure him to resist the demands from Axis governments. The canal must remain open."

Vale nodded. "Damned right. Do you think he'll sign the agreement?"

"I do," Hayden replied. "Assuming we pay him off with a one-billion-dollar development deal and commit to some peace keeping troops."

Vale frowned. "How's that going to land with President Dearing?"

Hayden made a face. "Alice won't like it. But she's a realist. And she knows how important a free canal is. I'll call her once we're in the air."

Hayden was on his second bourbon by the time the plane reached a cruising altitude of 30,000 feet. Panama City, Panama was about 1,500 miles away, and the trip was scheduled to take 4 hours.

The conversation with President Dearing was scrambled up, down and sideways. Reception was clear, and so was her response. "I'll tell you what, Al... If you can secure the canal for a billion dollars, that'll be a bargain. I'm all in."

It was a good call. And with that out of the way Hayden retired to the center section of the plane which consisted of a changing area, private lavatory, and a divan that had already been converted into a bed. A traveling photo of Hayden's wife, his daughter, and his son-in-law had been placed next to the daybed. His grandchildren Alex and Olivia had their own photo. They were smiling.

Hayden killed the light, turned over onto his left side,

and closed his eyes. Sleep pulled him down.

The Hoku Laser Facility, Bayingolin Mongol Autonomous Prefecture, China

Sunlight glittered off 500 solar panels, parabolic antennas were aimed at the sky, and most staff members were eating breakfast. But not the scientists in Building C. They'd been up for hours preparing to assassinate Vice President Al Hayden.

The project, code named *Xifang Guaiwu* (Western Monster), had been in the works for months—and was the brainchild of People's Liberation Army General Liu Jun.

Although the effort that made the project possible had begun years earlier, when the Hoku Laser Facility started to test lasers as possible weapons—culminating in the creation of a 50-100kW laser.

Buildings with retractable roofs had been constructed at Hoku so lasers could range, dazzle and even blind satellites as they passed over China. Activities that soon drew the ire of other countries who lodged complaints. All of which were ignored.

Over time, and consistent with certain internal reforms, the People's Liberation Army moved the program to the new PLA Aerospace Force, which had responsibility for testing rockets, missiles, and satellites. And now, inside Building C, all those years of effort were about to pay off. *Or*, Laser Technician Yuan Huang thought, *we'll miss. And General Liu Jun will have us shot.*

The men most likely to be shot along with Huang-included Laser Operator Zichen Wang, and Laser Systems Engineer Runchu Chen, who was supervising the last-minute adjustments that were necessary prior to a kill. Vice President Hayden was slated to be the first human targeted by the orbital weapon—named *Zhang Jian* (Long Sword). And that, in Huang's view, was an honor.

The key to the assassination was accurate information regarding the exact location, to

within a foot or two, of what the *gwailou* (westerners) called "Air Force Two," a plane traveling at approximately 500 miles per hour.

Such information would have been nearly impossible to obtain had it not been for

American websites like ADSBExchange.com, FlightRadar24.com, and FlightAware.com.

These sites used privately owned sensors to capture the movements of commercial and military aircraft 24 hours a day. That included military planes, special operations planes and yes, the VIP aircraft that carried the president, vice president and members of Congress.

All were equipped with FAA mandated ADS-B (Automatic Dependent Surveillance-Broadcast) transponders, which were available to anyone who had an internet connection.

That meant Vice President Hayden was about to be killed using information provided by his own government! An irony that caused Huang to smile.

"Huang," Chen said. "Run a check on the uplink, and run the final on Long Sword."

Huang was seated in front of a computer screen. One of twelve in the control room, all dark except for his, because there was no need for other techs to be present—and security was paramount. As his fingers typed, Huang's eyes checked the code for errors. His brain concluded that the connection to the satellite was intact.

Of equal importance was the fact that the target had been acquired by the correct satellite, and Long Sword was ready to fire. "The system is ready," Huang said simply.

There were three people in the control room, and perfect silence reigned. All eyes were on Chen as he said, "Fire."

Aboard Air Force Two over El Salvador, Central America

Vice President Hayden was in bed when the laser struck and threw him into a wall. He fell, hit his head, and immediately lost consciousness.

Pilot Lieutenant Colonel Lester Payton was sipping coffee when something hit the starboard wing, tore the engine off, and caused massive damage to the slats and flaps.

The loss of power and control surfaces put the two-engine C-32 into a dive and splashed hot coffee onto Payton's lap. He battled to regain control as a host of alarms sounded, while copilot Captain T.L. Jones flipped switches and spoke to the passengers. "Buckle your seatbelts and prepare for a crash. We're going down."

That was true. But *why?* Air Force Two was equipped with all sorts of gear that should have detected and jammed an incoming missile.

It didn't matter. What was, was. Payton's job was to find a place to land or, more accurately, to crash. They still had 20,000 feet of altitude to work with. But the ground was coming up fast. And, except for a scattering of lights, it was dark below. What a fucked-up way to die.

The deck was slanted down as Secret Service Agent Edward Kenny, Personal Aide Tom Seaver, and Special Advisor Jorge Ortiz battled to enter Hayden's private compartment.

Kenny swore when he saw the blood. He felt for a pulse and found one. Thank God. "Put him back on the bed .... Maybe it will cushion him when we hit."

By working together, the men managed to heave Hayden up onto the bed. Kenny threw himself on top of the vice president's body. "Use the blanket! Strap us down!"

The other men did the best they could, and were still working on it, when the 155-foot-long plane hit, took to the air, and hit again. Then the fuselage turned, struck the base of a cell tower, and broke in two.

The forward section bucked, throwing Kenny and the Vice President up against the ceiling. They landed on the bed. Neither one of them moved.

The Hoku Laser Facility, Bayingolin Mongol Autonomous Prefecture, China

Huang stared at the screen. "The plane's transponder is still broadcasting. And it's stationary."

A *cheer* went up. And there was reason to be jubilant. The enemy plane was down! It had to be if the transponder was stationary. And that suggested a crash.

But Laser Systems Engineer Runchu Chen was a cautious man. He knew that General Liu Jun wouldn't be satisfied with a downed aircraft. No, nothing less than a public admission of Hayden's death would satisfy Jun. The waiting began.

Near the village of Puebla, El Salvador

Due to Agent Kenny's sacrifice, and the efforts of a dozen survivors, Vice President Hayden was still alive. Not so the plane's pilots and 33 other people, only some of whom had been dragged free of the burning wreckage.

And, thanks to light provided by the fire, Secret Service Agent Chris Cole could see that the Air Force pilots had managed to put the C-32 down on an empty soccer field. It was nothing less than a fucking miracle.

That said, the situation sucked. They were on the ground in a nation known for its lawlessness. And, judging from the presence of a soccer field, very close to a village or town. Sirens could be heard in the distance as Cole rallied the survivors.

"Grab the stretcher and follow me! We need to get the hell out of here."

Press Secretary Margo Allen frowned. *"Why?"*

"Because this country is home to every kind of criminal there is," Cole replied. "All of whom would like to capture the Vice President. Let's go."

Hayden was wrapped in a blanket, and being carried on a folding stretcher, as Cole led the rest of them into the surrounding darkness. Air Force Two was down.

Soto Cano Air Base, Honduras

Joint Task Force-Bravo operated out of a Honduran military installation called Soto Cano Air Base, which was located in central Honduras. And, as Commanding Officer, Colonel James Patterson had responsibility for more than 500 U.S. military personnel, one of whom was a pain in the ass named Captain Jim Brody. But he, unfortunately, was the man Patterson needed to visit.

A light utility vehicle (LUV) was waiting for Patterson as he left the headquarters building. The sun was starting to rise in the east, and the air was humid as the driver wound his way through the maze of orange roofed buildings and came to a stop in front of the U.S. Army Stockade, or what the troops called "The Slammer."

"Wait for me," Patterson said. "I won't be long."

The driver nodded.

The sergeant manning the front desk stood and hollered, "Atten-shun!" as Patterson entered the reception area.

"As you were," Patterson said. "I'm here to visit Captain Brody. Is he in?"

It was a joke, and a good one. The noncom laughed. "Yes, sir.... The captain is present and accounted for. I can't leave the desk. Please hold while I get an escort."

The sergeant made a call. And while he waited Patterson reviewed the circumstances of Brody's arrest. It was a simple matter really .... The kind of thing that happened near military bases all around the world.

Brody was off duty, in town, and leaving a bar when he heard a woman scream and went to investigate. What he found was a Honduran noncom trying to rip a woman's top off. And not just any soldier, but a corporal who Brody recognized as one of his people.

So, he hit the assailant and knocked the man down. Mission accomplished. That's what Brody thought.

The locals didn't agree. Honduran MPs piled onto Brody, savaged the officer, and hauled him away. Brody said there was a knife. The Hondurans said there wasn't. Who to believe?

A corporal arrived. "Sir, please follow me."

The noncom led Patterson down a hallway with cells on the left. Only two were occupied. Brody was in the second, hanging from a water pipe, doing chin-ups. He had big arms, a lean torso, and muscular legs.

The corporal said, "Atten-shun!" and Brody dropped to the floor. His flip-flops made a *slapping* sound as they hit the concrete.

Patterson turned to the corporal. "Thanks. Open the cell and take a break."

The noncom was surprised and did nothing to hide it.

Brody was still at attention as Patterson entered the cell and sat on a concrete bench. "At ease. Take a seat."

The only other place to sit was on the opposing bench. Brody sat, wiped his chest with an olive drab towel, and nodded. "Good morning, Colonel. This is an unexpected pleasure."

"You won't think so once our conversation is over," Patterson replied.

Brody wiped the back of his neck. He didn't look scared. Just curious. "Okay, what's up?"

"Time is of the essence," Patterson replied. "So, I'm going to keep this short. Air Force Two crashed west of here, in El Salvador. We know that because the plane's transponder is still on. You're going to lead the extraction team."

Brody's eyebrows rose. "So, there are survivors?"

"We don't know," Patterson confessed. "We hope so. But understand this … If the Vice President is alive, he would be a very valuable prisoner to any number of criminal gangs, never mind members of the Axis."

Brody nodded. "Why me?"

"You're the best I have," Patterson replied. "Even if you are a gigundo pain in the ass. Your team will include three squads, one American, and two Honduran."

Brody frowned. "Honduran?"

"Yes," Patterson answered. "This is a *joint* task force, re-member? Plus, you trained them, they're bilingual, and they haven't forgotten the Football War."

Brody knew that the brief "Football War," or *Guerra del Futbol*, had been triggered by rioting in connection with the 1970 FIFA World Cup qualifier. But the dispute actually ran deeper than that. So, if called upon to fight El Salvador-ian gangs, the Hondurans would do so.

"Lieutenant Kelly is pulling the squads together and briefing them," Patterson added. "The platoon will be ready by the time you arrive at the helipads. We'll swing by the BOQ to grab your gear. Welcome to Operation Eagle," Patterson added. "You're Eagle-Six."

The White House, Washington D.C.

The Situation Room was located on the ground floor in the West Wing of the White House. Everyone stood as President Alice Dearing entered the room and promptly waved them back into their seats. Her chair was positioned at the head of a long table.

The attendees included Secretary of State Andy Boyko, Secretary of Defense Marvin Hoffman, Deputy Secretary of Defense for Intelligence and Security Mindy Corson, Dear-ing's Chief of Staff Mara Joy, and Press Secretary Ted Lowe.

"I'd like to say 'Good morning,' but that would be a lie," Dearing said. "As you know, Air Force Two is down somewhere in El Salvador, and the Vice President is missing.

"Let's go around the table. Mindy? What have you got?"

"We spotted the wreckage, Madam President. The night photos aren't very good, but new imagery will be available soon. It looks like the pilots tried to put down in a soccer field near a small town. The debris field is huge …. Numerous bodies are visible, but we haven't been able to identify any of them so far."

Dearing nodded. "Keep trying. Andy? What have you heard from our friends in El Salvador? When are they going to secure the crash site?"

Boyko scowled. "What friends? The people in San Salvador are too busy trying to stop the latest gang war to do much else. I hope to have something for you by noon."

Dearing scribbled a note. "Okay, Marvin…. Please tell me that our people in Honduras are on deck." Dearing was a graduate of the Naval Academy and had a tendency to use navy slang.

The SecDef nodded. "Yes, ma'am. Troops from Joint Base Bravo are in the air, and on the way. I'll keep you in the loop."

"Well," Dearing said, as her eyes roamed the faces in front of her. "Who was responsible?"

Mindy Corson cleared her throat. "That's a work in progress, Madam President. We know that while Air Force Two took a hit, we don't think it was from a surface to air missile."

Dearing frowned. "Why not?"

"I'll take that one," Hoffman said. "Because like Air Force One, Two was equipped with jammers designed to disrupt missile guidance systems. So, a SAM seems unlikely."

"Then, what does that leave?" Dearing inquired.

"Something new," Corson put in. "Something we don't have defenses for."

"Understood," Dearing replied. "Stay on it."

"Okay," Dearing added. "Last but not least, we have to accept that Al could be dead."

Chief of Staff Mara Joy nodded. "I'm working on arrangements just in case."

Dearing sighed, looked down, and up again. "All right… Let's move on. It's a big war. How many people did we lose yesterday?"

The city of San Salvador, El Salvador

Rico Salazar was asleep on a gigantic bed comprised of two king sized mattresses. He was flanked by two girls, both in their teens, with a dog curled up near his feet. It suddenly came to life, jumped up, and started barking.

Salazar, pistol in hand, sat up. His *segunda al mando* (second in command) was standing near the door, hands raised. "It's me, *Jefe* (boss). Don't shoot." The dog turned to lick itself.

Salazar lowered the gun. "What's wrong with you Manuel? It's eight am."

"I have news," Manuel said importantly.

"Well?" Salazar demanded. "What the fuck is it?"

"A plane crashed," Manuel replied. "Out near Puebla. A plane carrying the Vice President of the United States."

Manuel paused at that point, knowing Salazar would need some time to process the information and react to it.

Salazar frowned. "How the fuck do you know that?"

Manuel smiled. "I know that because it's on the police frequency. And the *chontes* (police) are trying to get their shit together."

Salazar swung his feet over onto the tile floor. It was cold. "Could he be alive?"

Manuel shrugged. "Who knows? But what if he is?

What would the Americans pay for him?"

Salazar grinned. "Good thinking, *compadre*. No wonder I keep you around. Let's load up. We're going to Puebla."

Saying it was easy. Doing it wasn't. First, it was necessary for Salazar to wake his *vatos* (gangsters) with a series of phone calls. Then Manuel had to gather the men together, fuel the gang's vehicles, and gun up. Headlights lit the scene as Salazar arrived.

"Okay, listen up! An Americano plane crashed. The Vice President of the United States might be aboard. And he would be worth a lot of money if we can capture him.

"That's the good news. The bad news is that the crash took place near Puebla. And, in order to get there, we'll have to pass through *territorio* controlled by MS-13."

Salazar's gang members hated Mara Salvatrucha, or MS-13, because they were affiliated with the famous 18th Street Gang, which had been at war with 13 for a long time. So, *growls* were heard, along with shouts of "Fuck them up!" and "*Esto es guerra!*" (This is war!)

Salazar nodded approvingly and waved his men toward the menagerie of vehicles. They were decorated with tiger stripes, as was fitting for a gang named the *Tigres*.

Engines *roared*, exhaust fumes spewed from exhaust pipes, and Salazar led the way. The gang leader prided himself on what he believed to be good looks, a quick mind, and an innate ability to strategize. That's why the column of vehicles soon split in two, with Manuel leading a feint to the northeast, so as to distract MS-13, while Salzar slipped past the opposing gang and entered Puebla. Would the ruse work? Both men were betting their lives on it.

The village of Puebla, El Salvador

There was reason to worry. There had been very little time in which to prepare. The departure from Soto Cano Air Base had been rushed and Captain Jim Brody knew that was the wrong way to launch a mission. Any mission, never mind one tasked with rescuing the Vice President of the United States. But, as Colonel Patterson put it, "Perfection is the enemy of getting shit done." Words to die by.

Brody ordered the helicopters to circle the crash site prior to landing. There were two reasons for that. The first was to disperse the looters, which it did, and the second was to look for any sign of an ambush. It didn't take an NTSB investigator to see that Air Force Two had broken in half. Pieces of wreckage lay everywhere, some still smoldering, as the helicopter rotors stirred the smoke.

If Brody had learned anything during his tour in Syria, it was that even the most innocent scene could conceal hidden dangers. So, it was important to focus. And two circuits of the area were required before Brody ordered two Black Hawks to land. Meanwhile the third helo continued to circle overhead where it could observe the surrounding terrain and provide fire support if necessary.

Brody was the first soldier out the door. And, as the others hit the ground, he was shouting orders. Not because his soldiers hadn't been told what to do, but because Brody believed in the old axiom: "Tell 'em. Tell 'em again. And tell 'em what you told 'em."

"Stick with your buddy! Watch for IEDs! Photograph each body. Collect DNA. And leave souvenirs alone. They might kill you."

Brody had seen some horrible things in Syria, including the aftermath of a terrible helicopter crash, but nothing to match the hellscape around him. Bodies, and parts of bodies were scattered about, mixed in with items stolen from the wreckage and left behind when the helos arrived.

The modified 757 had struck the ground nose first, collapsing the cockpit, and killing the pilots. The starboard engine was missing, but nowhere to be found, suggesting that it had been destroyed prior to impact.

There was no fire, which Brody considered to be something of a miracle, since he could smell jet fuel. And, had locals been allowed to get closer, some idiot might have dropped a cigarette onto the Jet-A soaked ground.

Brody noticed that an overwing hatch was open—which suggested that at least one passenger had escaped. If so, *who?* And where the hell were they? One possibility was that the survivor or survivors were among the dead bodies found adjacent to the plane.

But Brody figured it was equally possible that some passengers had survived, and fled the crash site, fearful of being captured. If so, was Vice President Hayden among them? His body hadn't been found, so there was reason to hope.

The air grew warmer as the sun continued to rise, and eventually turned muggy, which was typical for that time of year. What *wasn't* typical was the increasingly noticeable odor of rotting flesh. More helos had arrived by then. Most of the bodies had been removed, but Brody was under orders to collect debris as well, since the crash site was far from being secured.

And according to instructions from the Pentagon, investigators would want to see, feel, and touch anything that might shed light on how the plane had been shot down.

That made sense to Brody, but not to a Honduran major, who understood the need to "Collect rubbish" as he put it, but thought the other two Black Hawks were unnecessary.

"Here's the problem, sir," Brody said. "If I release those helos, and we're attacked while the others are gone, what then? The extra Hawks are our way out of here. And *your* way out of here, so long as you're on the ground. Capeesh?"

The Honduran didn't know what "capeesh" meant, but he got the idea.

Finally, with the sun high in the sky, Brody boarded the last helo out. Villagers shaded their eyes, waited for the

Hawk to clear the area, then rushed to recover what they could.

Brody waved his RTO (radio telephone operator) to the back of the cabin and took the handset. "Nest, this is Eagle-Six. Recovery mission complete. No sign of Chicago. Returning to base. Over."

✪

"Chicago" was Hayden's code name. Colonel Patterson didn't know what to feel. Sadness? Because there was a good chance that the Vice President was dead? Or hope? Because he might be alive? There was a bottle of Maker's Mark in a desk drawer. A present from his wife. It was time to pop the cork.

The village of Puebla, El Salvador

Fortunately, Manuel had been able to distract enough MS-13 assholes that Salazar's *soldados* (soldiers) had been able to fight their way through two of the opposing gang's roadblocks plus a police checkpoint.

But a price had been paid. Four of Salazar's men had been killed, and six had been wounded, two seriously. They were currently on their way to a hospital in the back of a much-needed gun truck. And that was an absolutely necessity in order to maintain morale.

However, as a result of these delays, the *Tigres* had arrived too late to loot the plane, much less capture the American politician. So, Salazar was forced to stand there and watch as the last helicopter took off, turned away, and quickly disappeared. *Mierda.* (Shit.)

Salazar was about to board his truck when a *segundo al mando* named Paco stopped him. "A local man would like to speak with you, *Jefe.*"

The man in question was standing a respectful distance away, his head bare, with hat in hands. Salazar frowned. "Tell him to eat shit and die. I'm going home."

Paco mustered his best smile. "With all due respect, *Jefe*... I think you should speak with him. His name is Lorenzo. He herds goats. And last night, after the crash, he saw some *extranjeros* (foreigners) leave the area."

Salazar smiled crookedly. "You never cease to amaze me Paco, and you never cease to piss me off. Why not tell me what Lorenzo said right off the top?"

"Because," Paco replied mischievously, "it's more fun this way."

Salazar couldn't help but smile. "You're going to go too far one of these days, Paco, and I'm going to shoot you."

Paco nodded agreeably. "Of course. That's to be expected."

Salazar tried to muster a smile as he approached Lorenzo. "*Buenas noches, señor*. You saw some foreigners leave the area. Please tell me more."

"There were six, maybe seven of them," Lorenzo replied. "And one of them had to be carried."

Salazar felt a sudden surge of hope. Maybe, just maybe, a very important payday was in the offing. "Thank you, Lorenzo. Would you be so kind as to accept this twenty-dollar bill? And lead us to the spot where the *extranjeros* are hiding?"

Lorenzo made the twenty disappear. "I can't be certain where they are hiding *El Jefe*, but I know where I would hide. And that's in the old winery."

"Excellent," Salazar replied. "And don't worry. If they aren't where you think they'll be, no harm will come to you."

Lorenzo's expression brightened, and he set off in a northerly direction, with the *Tigres* following behind him.

Salazar was expecting a short walk. But it soon became apparent that their destination was some distance away. Finally, at the point where Salazar was feeling winded and estimated he had walked a mile, a vine-covered tower appeared in the distance.

That was when Paco ordered the *miembro de una pandilla* (gang members) to stop and take cover. He then gathered together a five-man team and proceeded to lead them forward through an area of tall grass, along a stone wall, and under a wooden arch.

From there it was necessary to belly crawl through a tangle of berry vines to a point where a gaping hole offered the view of a clearing beyond. "Come," Paco whispered. "We'll surprise them."

✪

Seven Americans were hiding in the old winery along with Vice President Hayden, who was conscious, but bleary. The group included Secret Service Agent Chris Cole, Agent Al Mundy, Chief of Staff Emory Vale, Personal Aide Tom Seaver, Special Advisor for the Western Hemisphere Jorge Ortiz, and Press Secretary Margo Allen.

Cole, who had emerged as the group's leader, was worried. Black Hawk helicopters had been passing overhead all morning, but *whose*? Friendlies were a possibility. But not the *only* possibility. Did the El Salvadorian government have Black Hawks? That wasn't out of the question since the U.S. had allowed various countries to buy them.

But, even if they did, should he regard the Salvadorians as friendly? Ortiz cautioned against it. "It's a tossup as to whether El Salvador is a dictatorship or a democracy. So, if we hand the boss over, there's no way to know what they'll do with him."

As a result, the fugitives were frozen in place. And not just frozen in place, but thirsty, and increasingly hungry. Somebody had to go for help. Ortiz would be best, since he spoke Spanish—and had a better understanding of the culture than anyone else in the group.

That's what Cole was thinking when Seaver called down from the tower. "Men with guns! They're outside!"

Mundy pulled his nine and rushed to the hole in the

building's west flank. A burst of gunfire struck Mundy's chest, but failed to put him down, thanks to his body armor.

The agent fired his pistol, staggered as bullets struck his legs, and collapsed.

Cole rushed to help, killed the first man to enter through the hole, and was lining up for another shot when someone fired at him through an open window. The bullet struck Cole's temple, blood flew, and he collapsed.

Margo Allen went to retrieve Cole's pistol but stopped when a man entered and fired into the dirt floor. His English was adequate but no more than that. "I am Paco…. Stop! We kill all of you? Or you live. We get Vice President either way."

Ortiz raised his hands. "Hand Vice President Hayden over to the American embassy. They will reward you."

"Or," Salazar said, as he left the shadows, "we can auction Señor Hayden off, and make millions of U.S. dollars. *Me*? I vote for option two."

CHAPTER TWO

Washington DC, the White House

IN contrast with the day before, the Situation Room was full to overflowing with government officials, senior military officers, and staff members.

Once everyone was seated, President Dearing looked around the room. "You know why we're here. The Vice President was captured by a gang called the *Tigres*, led by a shithead named Rico Salazar. He posted a message on the *Tigre* website a few hours ago. Roll the tape please."

Video monitors were mounted on opposite walls. The footage had obviously been shot with a cell phone, and the lighting was poor, but all of them could see the man slumped forward on a straight-backed chair with his chin resting on his chest.

A chorus of gasps were heard as a tattooed man stepped into the frame, took hold of Hayden's hair, and pulled the vice president's head back. Hayden blinked. His eyes were out of focus, his face was badly bruised, and his clothes were filthy.

"There," the man said. "You see, Americans? You see, Russians? You see, Isis? We have him. And if you want him, then submit the highest bid, and he's yours! You can contact me through this website." The video dumped to black.

"Sickening, isn't it?" Dearing inquired. "All right—let's get down to business. First, is there anyone in this room who questions that man's identity? Because the conspiracy assholes are hawking their bullshit online." Silence reigned.

Dearing nodded. "Okay, priority one is to pull Al out of there. We'll pay if we have to, but I for one would like to snatch Albert, and kill a lot of bad people in the process.

"But, in order to do that, we need to know where he is. And our best people are working the problem. In the meantime, the press is going bonkers, as they should—and Ted Lowe will be in charge of that. Ted, what's the plan?"

Press Secretary Ted Lowe stood. "We opened a 24/7 news desk where reporters can get the latest. We plan to hold two pressers a day, and we're going to rely on many of you to provide reassuring blah-blah as needed." That produced some titters and smiles.

"Stay positive," Dearing added. "We're at war and good morale is critical."

"Finally, there's the matter of who shot Air Force Two down. Kyle? What have you got?"

Kyle Anderson was Director of the Central Intelligence Agency. He was known for his smarts, dedication, and colorful bow ties. He stood. "We theorize that the weapon used to bring Air Force Two down was something other than a SAM. First, because the plane's defensive systems would neutralize any missile the Salvadorians might launch.

"Second, because the Salvadoran government lacks a motive. And third, because we have a suspect with the means *and* a motive. And that's the Chinese."

A photo appeared on the screens. The man had droopy eyes, a downturned mouth, and was wearing a green uniform with three gold stars on each shoulder.

"Please allow me to introduce General Liu Jun," Anderson said. "He's in charge of the PLA Aerospace Force and, more specifically, three launch centers. That includes the *Jiuquan* Satellite Center located in Inner Mongolia. It's the main base for testing the Long Sword series of rockets, as well as other missiles and various satellites."

Anderson paused, as if to make sure that everyone was listening, before continuing. "Now, *this*," Anderson said as a photo appeared, "is a Chinese August 1 Medal …. The highest medal the People's Republic of China can bestow on a member of the military.

"According to law," Anderson continued, "and I quote: 'This medal is awarded to military personnel who have made great contributions, and established outstanding meritorious service in safeguarding national sovereignty, security, and development interests, and promoting the modernization of national defense and the military, and have had a profound impact on the country and the entire military.'

"So, why," Anderson demanded rhetorically, "did the People's Daily newspaper report that an obscure general, the man in charge of a testing facility in Mongolia, received the August 1 Medal yesterday?" The question was met with silence. But all of them knew the answer.

Soto Cano Air Base, Honduras

Captain Jim Brody was in his room at the BOQ, writing an after-action report, when there was a knock on the door. That was something of a formality since the door was partially open to facilitate the lackadaisical air conditioning.

Brody said, "Come," and turned to see Private Dean standing at attention. "At ease. What's up?"

"Sir, the CO wants to see you in his office."

Brody frowned. "I have a phone."

Dean was staring at a spot over Brody's head. "Sir, yes, sir. But you don't answer it."

Brody grinned. "Guilty as charged. Is there any chance that you'd write this report for me?"

"No, sir."

"Damn it. Okay, tell Colonel Patterson that I'll put some pants on, and hurry over. Dismissed."

After donning clean cammies, Brody left for the HQ building. The air was humid, and clouds were gathering, both of which suggested the likelihood of rain. And then, in keeping with its usual pattern, the sun would reappear shortly thereafter. Brody hoped so.

Soto Cano Air Base was a Honduran asset located five miles to the south of Comayagua, Honduras. It was home to more than 500 U.S. personnel, including the U.S. military's Joint Task Force-Bravo (JTF-B). Elements of the Honduran Air Force Academy were stationed there as well.

The *roar* of jet engines was heard as a C-17 thundered overhead, touched down, and the plane's thrust reversers came on. Such comings and goings were so common that Brody wasn't conscious of the landing. The orange roofed headquarters building had AC, and it was running full tilt, as Brody entered the reception area.

The NCO at the front desk waved Brody through. On his way towards Patterson's office Brody had to pass Rosa, the colonel's secretary. She smiled. "Is there something wrong with your phone?"

"Yes," Brody replied. "The damned thing rings all the time."

Rosa laughed. "A meeting is underway. The colonel is expecting you."

Brody made his way to the double doors, knocked, and heard Patterson say, "Enter!"

As Brody walked into the office, he saw that four people were seated at the colonel's round conference table. They included Patterson, the Honduran major that Brody had offended at the crash site, Captain Norman Gates, often referred to as "Gizmo" behind his back, and a Honduran army lieutenant. A female. And although increasingly common, that was still notable.

Patterson waved Brody towards a vacant chair and made the introductions. "I believe you met Major Gomez at the crash site. You know Captain Gates, and Lieutenant Perez is here on a special assignment. More on that shortly. As you arrived, the captain was sharing some very interesting intelligence."

Brody knew the comment was a slap on the wrist for being late.

Major Gomez was clearly pleased regarding the implied criticism and smiled thinly. Perez was largely expressionless. But Brody thought he saw a smile tugging at both corners of her mouth.

Gates nodded. "Yes, sir. Very interesting indeed. First, let me explain the problem. We know the vice president is being held by the *Tigres,* who are based in San Salvador. But, like most gangs they have dozens of crash pads, warehouses, armories and garages. And Hayden could be in any of them. Or none of them.

"So, our friends in Washington D.C. and the Honduran 3-1-6 Battalion went to work tracking the *Tigre* website to its geographical location. And, while the Tigs were smart enough to use a VPN (virtual private network) to mask their true location, our folks were able to use a tool called NordVPN Lookup, which tracked the *Tigre* IP address to its source."

"That's awesome," Brody exclaimed. "Let's go get him!"

Patterson nodded. "That's the right spirit. And I said as much. But the people in the Pentagon don't think that we're qualified to stage such a complex raid. That honor will go to a newly created organization called 'Oppo One.' Actually, Oppo One, Two, and Three—because there are multiple teams.

"Unlike SEAL Team Six, SAS (Special Air Service), and *Kommando Spezialkrafte* (German Special Forces), the

Oppo team members are drawn from *all* the Allied countries," Patterson explained. "And, according to what I've heard, they think they're the best of the best."

"I hope that's true," Brody said. "So how 'bout a two-day pass?"

Patterson shook his head. "Sorry, no pass for you. Captain Gates, with help from the folks who report to Major Gomez, are using a drone to keep an eye on the Tigres. But the Oppo staff wonks insist that we send a qualified officer in on the ground to look around and take pictures. That's you! Lieutenant Perez will serve as your interpreter. And, if it comes to that, your bodyguard."

Perez stared at Brody, as if daring him to object, but he didn't. "I look forward to working with the lieutenant. So, what about the Salvadorans? Are they in on this?"

"No," Gomez replied. "The government can't be trusted. That's one of the reasons gangs are so prevalent. And there are likely to be spies, right here, on this base. So don't tell anyone where you're going or why."

Patterson nodded. "That's right. We'll insert you tonight. You'll have fake ID cards, wear civilian clothes, and carry cell phones which will double as cameras."

Brody frowned. "Will I stick out?"

"No," Patterson replied. "About 12% of the Salvadoran population is white."

Perez eyed Patterson. "What about weapons?"

Gomez responded. "Pistols. Two each if you wish. You can draw them from the armory. No questions asked."

"Get some sleep," Patterson advised. "Both of you were scrubbed from the duty rosters as of an hour ago. I trust both of you know how to ride a motorcycle?"

Brody nodded, as did Perez. The meeting was over.

Brody stopped by the armory where, after reviewing what was available, he signed for a SIG Sauer 9mm M18 with two 17 round magazines, and a smaller Glock 26 "subcompact" nine plus two 10 round magazines.

If the armorer wondered why a line officer had need of a shoulder holster and an ankle holster, she managed to hide it.

A Salvadoran cell phone was waiting for Brody when he returned to the BOQ. A handwritten note came with it. "Select 'Bob' to reach us. P."

Brody checked and, sure enough, "Bob" was included on the list of contacts.

Thanks to the room's standard blackout shades, Brody was able to hit the rack and, much to his surprise, fell asleep immediately. His alarm went off at 0100.

After a quick shower he donned civilian clothes, grabbed a small knapsack, and made his way to the motor pool where a beat-up box truck was waiting. Perez was already there. She offered a helmet. "Try it."

It was too loose but the chin strap took care of the problem. "Thanks, Lieutenant. I'm Jim. What's your first name?"

"Maria. Just like my sisters."

"Your parents named all their daughters Maria?"

Perez smiled. "They thought it was funny."

"For them, maybe," Brody responded. "Where's our bike?"

Perez jerked a thumb back over her shoulder. "In the back of the truck."

"Okay. What is it?"

"It's a Yamaha XT250," Perez replied. "It looks newer than I'd like, but it will outrun the smaller engines that are typical around here."

Brody was impressed. Perez was not only paying attention to details, but clearly knew a thing or two about motorcycles. "So, who's going to sit up front?"

Perez grinned. "Thanks for asking. But, as you know, women normally ride in back unless they're alone. And we want to look normal."

That was true, and Brody was about to say so, when a man wearing a baseball hat approached them. The cap had the Honduras soccer team's logo printed on it. "Enter the truck, *por favor*. It's time to go."

Perez stared at him. "You're going to enter San Salvador wearing a Honduran soccer team hat? Are you loco? Give me that."

The driver handed the hat over and Perez tossed it into a shadow, then pointed at the cab. The driver obeyed.

After climbing aboard Brody was confronted with a wall of boxes, all labeled as being filled with bottles of *Sobresalir* palm oil. A narrow passage led into the "room" up front where the bike was. Brody checked the tie-downs. They were tight. "Fuel?"

"Full." Brody was falling in love.

Perez slapped the wall that separated them from the cab three times. The engine *roared*, the truck jerked ahead, and they were underway. The noise generated by the engine, and what sounded like a hundred loose parts, made it impossible to have a conversation.

So, there they sat, each with their own thoughts, as the truck paused at the main gate then *clattered* away.

Brody was reminded of a dark night in Syria. He'd been in the back of a truck then too, with members of the Free Syrian Army, on their way to attack a government radio station.

The objective had been simple. Destroy an ORTAS (the General Organization of Radio and TV) site and prevent it from spewing lies on behalf of the Bashar al-Assad regime.

And, as an American advisor, Brody wasn't expecting to play much of a role. The fighter in charge, a man named Omar Abadi, was a competent sort—and not one to rely on foreigners.

So, as Brody's CO put it, "Go in, stand around, and give

advice if asked. But Abadi's men will have the advantage of surprise and should be able to bring the tower down with a few sticks of dynamite. Boom! Mission accomplished."

Unfortunately, Captain Henry was wrong. Abadi's men *didn't* have the advantage of surprise because a government spy had gotten wind of the raid, and informed Bashar al-Assad's forces, who along with some Russians were lying in wait.

A fact that became apparent when an RPG hit the truck Brody was riding in. The force of the explosion tipped the vehicle over. At that point, half of the free army fighters were dead or wounded.

Then, as automatic weapons began to *rattle*, hundreds of bullets ripped through the canopy, and Abadi and another half-dozen men were killed.

Brody was dragging a fighter out of the truck, when a bullet hit the man in the head and blood splattered the floor.

Brody turned and was about to run, when a Russian soldier appeared. He pulled his pistol, shot the man three times, then wondered where his rifle was. Back where he'd been sitting, that's where. What a dumbass.

Voices arose nearby so Brody took shelter in a dry ditch then proceeded to belly crawl away. *Don't let the bastards take you. It would be better to bite the nine.*

That's what Brody was thinking as he squirmed into a culvert, felt for the PRC 160 radio, and thumbed it on. "Lifter-Three, this is Scarecrow. Force Five was ambushed short of the objective. Heavy casualties. Truck on fire south of my twenty. Will exfil to the north. Over."

The response came within seconds. "Scarecrow, this is Lifter-Three. We will engage to the south, turn, and pick you up. Continue to move north."

Brody heard, rather than saw the Black Hawk attack the government soldiers and felt sick to his stomach. Why was he alive? When so many, perhaps all of the other men in the truck, had been killed? It wasn't skill, that was for sure, nor was he particularly deserving. God definitely wasn't involved. So, what did that leave? Luck, that's what.

Was Vice President Hayden lucky too? Brody hoped so.

✪

Although the distance between the airbase and El Salvador wasn't that great, it took longer than Brody had expected, due to the need to grind up and over innumerable hills.

But, after what seemed like an eternity, the driver knocked on the wall.

Perez leaned in so that Brody could hear her. "We're coming up on a border crossing. It resembles a drive-thru barn. The Salvadoran border guards have seen this truck a thousand times. And they've been bribed a thousand times. So, we shouldn't have any trouble. But, if we do, kill them all." And with that Perez drew a retro M1911 .45.

Once again Brody was struck by her professionalism. Or was it pragmatism? "What's with the forty-five?"

"It belonged to my father," Perez replied, as if that explained everything. Then she brought a forefinger up to her lips.

It was midmorning by then. So, Brody could see the light that leaked through the wall of boxes when the rear doors were opened, and could hear some high-speed Spanish, as the driver talked shit and money changed hands.

Then the doors closed, the driver's side door slammed, and the truck jerked into motion. Perez made the 1911 vanish and offered a thumbs up.

Brody decided that Perez was pretty. With or without a pistol.

San Salvador awaited.

The Beidaihe Beach Resort, on China's Bohai Sea coast

Thanks to its location just 180 miles east of Beijing, the Beidaihe Beach Resort was a favorite with Chinese officials, and was well known as the Chinese Communist Party's summer retreat. As such, it was the site of frequent conferences and was, according to one American diplomat, "China's smoke-filled room." Especially with a war raging.

But being an official wasn't enough to earn an invitation to enjoy the resort's beautiful beach, warm water, and lush vegetation.

No, in order to visit, it was necessary to *be* somebody. And General Liu Jun, the man credited with shooting Air Force Two down, definitely qualified.

Jun loved to swim and was determined to take full advantage of his celebrity status. So, while his wife paid a visit to the resort's spa, he ventured down a secluded path to the beach and an area where his portly body was less likely to be noticed.

But that strategy didn't shield Jun from the watchful sensors of a high-flying "Wraith" drone and its aerial reconnaissance equipment.

So, when Jun happened to look up, a photograph of him was passed to a satellite, and from there to Washington D.C. That's where his identity was confirmed, a sanction was approved, and orders went out. All within the blink of an eye.

Jun was putting his snorkel on as the order was received by a U.S. submarine, which started a countdown. Then, when a blunt finger pushed a button, a Tomahawk cruise missile shot up out of the East China Sea and raced away. Jun was only waist deep in the warm water when the American weapon hit him. There was a flash of light, followed by a loud *boom*, as the general exploded. His snorkel was found on the beach.

La Comapania Azucarera de tres Hermansos, San Salvador (The Three Brothers Sugar Company, San Salvador)

Vice President Al Hayden was lying on a cot, eyes mostly closed, plotting his escape. The blurred vision had abated somewhat, as had the dizziness and the mental fog. The headache remained however, throbbing away.

His captors weren't aware of these improvements though, because Hayden had gone to great lengths to conceal his actual condition. And the subterfuge was working.

Although the guards were alert at first, Hayden's apparent inability to do little more than hobble to the bathroom caused the *Tigris* to relax. Because of that, Hayden planned to escape, and to do so before the gang could put him up for auction.

Except for a man named Pedro, the *deposito* (warehouse) was momentarily empty of people, and Hayden knew that was the best situation he could hope for. So, he groaned and raised an unsteady hand.

"*Hmph*," Pedro grunted, as he approached the cot. "The gringo needs to pee. Well, come on, let's get it over with."

Pedro helped Hayden to stand and, with one arm around his shoulder, the *pandillero* (gang member) assisted Hayden across the room to what had once been an employee bathroom.

Hayden was apprehensive. Could he do what needed to be done? He wasn't a man of violence. In fact, his wife referred to him as "my teddy bear." But he had to try.

The *bano* smelled like what it was—a lavatory that hadn't been cleaned in a long time. The stench made Hayden nauseous.

Once the prisoner was positioned in front of a urinal, Pedro turned his back and lit a hand rolled cigarette. Based on previous experience, Pedro knew the smoke would help to dispel the stink. That's what Pedro was thinking when the improvised noose dropped over his head and tightened around his throat.

The belt had been a Christmas present from Hayden's daughter. Never in a thousand years would she have imagined her father using it to choke a man to death. Yet that's exactly what Hayden planned to do.

The cigarette *hissed* as it landed on the wet floor. Pedro clawed at the leather band, his face turned blue, and his vision started to fade. Then he threw himself sideways, taking Hayden down as well. The gambit failed. His lungs tried to suck in air without success. *Salazar will be angry*, Pedro thought. *I hope he doesn't ...* Darkness took him in.

Hayden released the body and struggled to stand. His clothes smelled like pee. Once on his feet Hayden bent over, chest heaving, as he battled to breathe. *Get moving*, he told himself, *before they find you.*

Hayden straightened his back, ordered his feet to move, and shuffled to the swinging door. It opened slowly, as if reluctant to let him go.

But he managed to pass through. Sunlight streamed down between holes in the roof, and wings fluttered somewhere above, as Hayden stumbled toward what might be a door to the outside.

He was halfway there when it opened, a *pandillero* appeared, and stopped to stare. "*Que carajo?*" (What the fuck?)

Attack him, Hayden thought. *Knock him down.* He tried, but the vertigo was back, and the cement floor came up to smack him. The world faded to black.

San Salvador, El Salvador

The situation in San Salvador was bad, very bad, and that made it difficult to travel even short distances. Most of the combatants had established roadblocks, including government soldiers, gang members, and vigilantes.

However, as awful as things were, all of the groups had one thing in common—they wanted dollars. American dollars. Ones were fine. In fact, to offer anything larger than that was to set one's self up for trouble.

Thanks to Perez's foresight, the couple had ones—lots of them—which she doled out along with bursts of rapid-fire Spanish.

Brody didn't know what the Honduran was saying, but whatever it was worked, and there was only one occasion when someone tried to stop them. That someone was a vigilante.

And, when the *pistolero* made a grab for the handlebars, Perez leaned to the right and shot him. The man went down.

Brody opened the throttle. The bike bumped over the body, another vigilante fired, and Perez turned to empty her magazine while the motorcycle pulled away.

Brody knew the helmets were wired, but the voice still came as a surprise. "Nice work," Gates said. "My drone caught the whole thing. Hayden is being held in a warehouse located in District 5. That's one of the most crime-ridden sections of San Salvador. I'll guide you."

Both Brody and Perez had thin boom mikes. "Now you show up," Brody said. "Where were you fifteen minutes ago?"

"I was eating breakfast," Gates replied.

During the next twenty minutes Brody was directed through a complicated series of twists and turns as the shacks where most people lived gradually gave way to shuttered shops, graffiti covered walls, and empty-eyed windows.

"You're getting close," Gates advised. "Start looking for a place to hide the bike. Otherwise, someone will sure as hell steal it."

Brody spotted a partially burned out building up ahead. "How's our six?"

Perez turned to look. "Our six is clear," she assured him.

"I agree," Gates offered.

Brody turned onto a walkway, took his feet off the pegs, and bumped his way over pieces of fire-blackened debris until he passed through what had been a doorway. Then he braked.

There was no roof. But, with walls all around, it seemed unlikely that the motorcycle would be spotted from the ground. As for the air above, that was another thing entirely. "What do you think, Perez? *Si*, or *no*?"

"*Si*," Perez said, as she backed off the seat. "How close are we?"

"About a block away," Gates answered. "Leave your helmets with the bike. But bring the radio and use the Bluetooth earbuds.

"Remember to turn your phone cams on and stay hidden—to the extent that such a thing is possible. How you get the shots is up to you …. But what we're looking for is the kind of stuff drones can't capture without being spotted. Doors, guards, heavy weapons—all at street level. I'll make suggestions from time to time. Over."

Brody checked to make sure that his phone was on and the camera was working. Perez's brown eyes locked with his. "Let's work as a team," she suggested. "I'll take the photographs, while you provide security. Are you okay with that?"

Brody nodded. "Let's do it."

After leaving the building, a few steps took them out onto a badly cracked sidewalk next to a narrow street. Brody turned left and rounded a corner, with Perez at his side. What had once been a mini-mall was to their left and offered an opportunity to duck out of sight.

The nearest entrance to the mall was by way of "Rosa's Nail Salon." The door hung askew and offered an easy way in.

Sunlight slanted down through a huge hole in the roof, and wings flapped, as they passed through the nail salon and entered the inner courtyard. Glass *crunched*, and pieces of wood *snapped*, as Brody moved forward. Then a horrible smell invaded his nostrils. And it wasn't long before the reason for that became obvious. There, dangling from one of the overhead beams were four corpses. A woman and three men.

Brody had the names and photos of Hayden's staff members on his phone. He brought them up. And sure enough, even though their faces had a blueish hue, it was evident that Margo Allen, Emory Vale, Tom Seaver, and Jorge Ortiz had been murdered. His stomach heaved.

As for why the Americans had been killed, Brody assumed it was because Hayden was the big fish, and the *Tigres* didn't think the vice president's aides were worth their time and energy.

Perez crossed herself and moved her lips as if in prayer.

It would have been nice to take care of the bodies in some way, but Brody and Perez didn't have the time or means to do so.

Finally, after entering what had been a barber shop, Brody was able to peer past some grimy blinds and see a building on the other side of the street. "That's the warehouse," Gates whispered. "Get what you can. Over."

Perez brought her phone up and began to click away. Guards bracketed the front door. Both were heavily armed. A gun truck was parked a few yards away to the west. There was no sign of a driver. But a man was seated next to the LMG (light machine gun) in the back, smoking a cigar.

Once the situation out front was documented, it was time to start the ticklish business of exiting the mini-mall and working their way east, into a low rent flop house. Perez led the way with her pistol hidden, asking each person she encountered if they'd seen her sister, who was rumored to be in the area.

Brody slipped his phone into a pocket, which not only served to hide it, but freed both hands to pull weapons if necessary.

The warehouse occupied most of a city block. It took some time for them to take a position opposite it, on the east side of the street. There weren't any entrances on the east side of the warehouse, just windows, all of which were located high up.

But, while Brody didn't see any guards at ground level, he did catch occasional glimpses of a man on the roof. Perez wasn't able to get a photo of him, due to the angle, but Gates assured her that his MQ-1C Gray Eagle drone could "see" the roof and record what it saw.

"The next one is going to be harder," Gates warned. "There's no cover on the southside. So, walk by, and pause for a photo with the guards. The kind of snapshot you might see on Instagram. But make sure the southside entrance is visible in the background. Over."

"Is that all?" Brody inquired sarcastically.

"Yup," Gates replied. "Thanks for asking. Over."

When they were about fifty feet away, a guard yelled at them and pointed toward the far side of the street. Perez replied with a request to have her picture taken with the gangsters.

The *pistoleros* liked that, and invited the pretty *chica* to approach them, striking a variety of manly poses while Brody took photos.

Then, after kissing each gang member on the cheek, Perez returned to Brody's side and they walked away. "Damn," Gates said. "That was awesome!

"Okay, take a right at the corner and walk north. There aren't any guards on that side of the warehouse, so no prob. Return to the bike, mount up, and head home. I'll guide you to the border. Over."

It was a plan. A good plan. Or would have been if the bike had been there. But it wasn't. Somehow, someway, the twosome had been spotted. As they left the burned-out house? Maybe. Not that it mattered.

A tiny mike was clipped to Brody's shirt. He spoke into the voice activated microphone. "The motorcycle is gone."

A long pause preceded Gates' reply. "Shit. Sorry about that. I was focused on the area around the warehouse."

"Do you have any suggestions?"

"Yes," Gates replied. "Email me all of your photos."

Perez aimed a middle finger up at the sky.

Brody cleared his throat. "And?"

"And return to the base," Gate said. "Keep us informed."

Brody frowned. "Norm? You're shitting me, right?"

There was no answer.

Brody looked at Perez as she hit "Send," and tucked her phone away.

They were on their own in a dangerous city. If Perez was frightened, Brody couldn't see any sign of it on her face. "Send your photos."

Brody smiled. "That's 'send your photos, sir.'"

Perez laughed. Brody liked the sound of it. "Okay," Perez replied. "Send your photos, *sir*. Or I will leave your gringo ass to reach Soto Cano on your own."

"I stand corrected," Brody replied.

The next couple of minutes were spent entering the email address they'd been given, selecting photos, and sending them off. "Okay? So now what?"

"Now," Perez replied, "we're going to head for my *abuela's* house."

Brody frowned. "Your grandmother's house? Why?"

"Because we can hide there," Perez replied. "While we wait for Tio Alberto. He drives a taxi. And he will take us to the base.

"Or," Perez added, "we can try to make it on foot. No worries, I'm sure you'll blend in."

Brody laughed. "All right, you win as usual. Please lead the way."

After leaving the burnt-out house Perez took his arm, the way a wife might, and steered him on a zigzagging course through a residential neighborhood. They paused now and then to purchase elements of a rudimentary disguise for Brody, and to look for any sign that they were being followed. So far, so good.

But, Brody thought, *when we reach the base, I'm going to find Gates and kick his ass.*

"We're halfway there," Perez announced, as they approached a footbridge that spanned a gully. As they crossed Brody saw that there was so much garbage below that a sluggish stream was barely able find a path through it.

"Uh oh," Perez said as they reached the middle of the span. "The Barrio 6 gang. Don't be fooled by the bats. They have guns too."

Brody registered a sense of alarm as a gang of scrawny teens filtered onto the far end of the bridge. Most were carrying baseball bats. Because they were headed for a game? Apparently not.

The teens had stopped. They were laughing and swinging their bats.

Brody turned to check his six. Five or six boys, also armed with bats, were approaching from behind. Brody could tell that the trap, because that's what it clearly was, had been used many times before.

He turned to Perez. "What would you suggest? Fire a shot in the air?"

"No," Perez said, as she pulled the .45. "Kill them! I'll take the ones on the left."

CHAPTER THREE

San Salvador, El Salvador

PEREZ began to fire the Colt 1911. *Boom! Boom! Boom!* A gang member fell with each shot. The rest scattered. Some drew pistols and fired back.

His companion's pistol had a seven-round magazine. Brody knew that. So, he held his fire until the seventh empty shell casing flew through the air.

Then, knowing Perez would have to reload, he fired two shots. Both were aimed at boys with pistols and both targets went down.

Brody whirled, and just in time too, because a teen with a ball bat was six feet away and running straight at him. He shot his assailant three times, causing the boy to stumble and fall. Brody was about to fire on gang members standing a short distance beyond the fallen teen, when they turned and ran. "Come on!" Perez shouted. "Follow me!"

Perez ran and Brody followed. They had to leap over bodies and pools of blood as they raced toward the east end of the bridge. *Sirens* could be heard by then, and Brody knew what would happen if he was arrested. He could imagine the headline. "Children massacred by American army officer!" And Perez wouldn't fare much better.

Once clear of the bridge, Perez led Brody into a maze of houses which grew increasingly prosperous as the incline steepened. The reasons for that were obvious. The air was slightly cooler, the homes had better views, and the sewage they produced ran downhill.

Brody was breathing heavily by the time Perez paused, returned the .45 to its holster and extended her hand. "We're lovers, out for a walk."

Brody stopped to take her hand and marveled at how small it was. "Your gun," Perez said. "Put it away."

"Yes, ma'am."

Perez smiled. "That's more like it."

Señora Camila Perez lived in a two-story house, safely tucked behind high walls, and protected by an iron gate. And when Perez pressed a button, and spoke into a metal grill, Brody heard a male voice. "Maria! Welcome home!"

Something *whirred*, the gate began to open, and the couple slipped through. A middle-aged man appeared. He was armed with a 12-gauge pump gun.

Perez kissed him on the cheek. "This is Captain Jim Brody. Jim, Mateo is my grandmother's driver, gardener and security guard."

Mateo nodded. "I heard shooting. And sirens."

Perez nodded. "We had a run in with the Barrio 6 gang."

There was a clang as the gate closed. "They get more aggressive with each passing day," Mateo said. "Don't worry, I will stand guard. Now go! Your grandmother heard your voice over the intercom. She'll be waiting."

Perez led the way. The path led to a formal entrance. A metal-strapped door opened onto a formal reception hall. And as Perez turned right, Brody followed her into a beautifully appointed great room complete with floor length drapes, sparkling chandeliers, and a large fireplace. Brody assumed it was rarely used given the climate.

Camila was seated in a corner, where the sunlight

splashed her face, and a walkie talkie was close at hand. Her hair was white, her face was ageless, and her voice was cultured. "Maria! Come, give me a kiss! Which Maria are you?" That was when Brody realized that Camila was blind.

"I'm Maria Tres" (three) Perez said, as she went over to kiss her grandmother's cheek. "And," Perez added, "I'm not alone. Army Captain Jim Brody is with me."

"Ahh, a capi-tan! Your father was a capi-tan before he was promoted to major. But that was a long time ago. Come here Capi-tan Jim and kiss an old woman's cheek."

Brody went over, and was about to kiss Camila's cheek, when her hands came up to capture his face. Then, using her thumbs, Camila explored Brody's nose, eyes, and cheeks.

"Yes," Camila said. "This is the one. You may kiss me."

Brody obeyed. And, as he withdrew, Camila took hold of her walkie talkie. "You will stay for dinner. I will tell Rosa, and she will prepare something special."

"I'm sorry," Perez said. "But we can't stay. We must return to the base as soon as possible. We need Tio Alberto to pick us up. I'm going to call him."

Perez made the call, leaving Brody to make small talk with Camila. Most of the conversation had to do with her dead husband's military career which, from the sound of it, was quite successful. *And that*, Brody concluded, *explains Maria's choice of professions and the Colt 1911.*

Tio Alberto arrived thirty minutes later. After saying goodbye to Camila, and promising to return for a dinner, Brody and Perez went out through the front gate. Mateo was there to see them off. "Be careful! See you soon!"

Alberto's taxi was a surprise. Rather than a Corolla, Civic, or Elantra it was a tank-like 1955 Buick, complete with a mouthlike grill, portholes on the front fenders, and four doors.

But that wasn't all. The vehicle was enclosed by an exoskeleton made from tubular steel— and that included the doors—making the Buick nearly unassailable.

Screens covered the side and back windows, so that it would be difficult, if not impossible, to throw a grenade into the interior. And if Brody wasn't mistaken, the beast was equipped with roll flat tires.

As for the Buick's owner, Alberto was sporting a straw Pork Pie hat, a tropical shirt, and reflective sunglasses which he removed to shake hands with Brody. "It's a pleasure to meet you Señor …. Don't worry, I will take you to the base unharmed. Everyone knows me, and I go where I please. Isn't that right, Maria?"

"It is," Maria agreed, as she kissed Alberto's cheek. "Let's hit the road."

Once in the back, on a seat wide enough for four, Brody felt more than secure as Alberto passed through roadblocks and checkpoints while dispensing one-dollar bills through a hole in the side window. Alberto was, it seemed, a combination fixture and folk hero. That left Brody free to think about things other than simply staying alive.

"So," Brody said, as he turned to Perez. "Your grandmother said, 'This is the one.' What does that mean?"

Perez shrugged. "Who knows? She's an old woman. She says lots of things none of us understand."

It was dark by then. And, after half an hour or so, Perez fell asleep. Gradually, in response to the car's movements, her head came to rest on Brody's shoulder. He liked the smell of her hair and the warmth of her body. His phone began to vibrate. Colonel Patterson? Captain Gates? Probably. Well, fuck them. Brody was busy.

Washington DC, the Oval Office

Dearing was seated behind the Resolute desk fiddling with a pen. Chief of Staff Mara Joy, and Press Secretary Ted Lowe sat facing her. "Well," Dearing said. "The Secretary of State informs me that yes, the President of El Salvador will allow emergency operations in San Salvador, if we forgive half a billion worth of debt and grant the country a most-favored-nation status. And we agreed to that on the condition that El Salvador drop its neutrality and join the Alliance.

"That means Oppo Three will be able to snatch Al without taking fire from the locals. And, theoretically, the Alliance is one nation stronger. Although we can't expect much help from a country largely controlled by gangs.

"So," Dearing added, "your note indicted that we have a problem with the *New York Times?*"

"Yes, ma'am," Lowe said. "Sam Waters read the piece to me over the phone. Most of the story is correct. A criminal enterprise has the vice president and plans to auction him off. That suggests a high-level leak. But be that as it may, Sam is looking for confirmation, plus an interview with you. And, if we refuse, he'll run the story anyway."

Chief of Staff Mara Joy nodded. "I suggest that we grant an interview, confirm the basics, but refuse to provide details while the situation is in flux. Waters will understand that."

"I agree," Dearing said. "Meanwhile, Oppo Three is enroute and, assuming they're successful, Al will be free in a matter of hours. We'll hold a press conference then."

"And if they fail?" Joy inquired.

Dearing shook her head. "I refuse to consider that. Get Waters on the phone."

Soto Cano Air Base, Honduras

Brody was present as nav lights appeared and the *roar* of helicopter engines was heard. The plan was for Oppo Three to land, receive a final briefing, and reboard for the flight to the warehouse where Hayden was being held.

That was both good and bad in Brody's opinion. Good, in that the sooner they could rescue the vice president the better, and bad since the special ops team was likely to be tired.

Dust blew in every direction as the helo put down, a door opened, and Colonel Patterson went forward to greet the newcomers. "Who are they?" Inspector Medina shouted over the noise.

Medina had arrived half an hour earlier and was, according to Patterson, the operation's liaison with El Salvador's government. Brody's job was to shepherd him around.

Why was Medina so late? That was above Brody's pay grade. But it appeared that some sort of deal had been done between the U.S. and El Salvador. Fortunately, Medina spoke excellent English.

"Oppo Three is a special operations team," Brody explained, as the engines continued to spool down. "It's new, so I don't have all of the background, but it's my understanding that the Oppo teams are drawn from crack military units throughout the Alliance. And they're trained to deal with situations like this one."

Medina nodded and said, "I see," although Brody doubted that was true.

Oppo Three consisted of six soldiers, all following Patterson as he led them over to where Brody and Medina stood. "It's my pleasure to introduce Inspector Medina," Patterson said. "He's our liaison with the El Salvadorian government. And this is Captain Brody. He shot some of the photos that were included in your briefing materials.

"Gentlemen, this is the Oppo Three's CO, code name Andre."

Brody shook Andre's hand. And, as their eyes met, Brody was struck by how dilated the other man's pupils were. Was Andre on so-called "Go pills?" The kind he had been required to use in Syria? If so, Oppo Three's CO wasn't going to be at his best.

"It's a pleasure to meet you," Andre said in a toneless voice. "And you," Andre added, as he shook Medina's hand. "You can relax now. Oppo Three is here. We will free the prisoner and return him to you." Then Patterson led him away. The other members of the Ops team nodded as they followed along behind.

"He seems quite confident," Medina commented.

Yes, Brody thought. *Too confident in my estimation. But who am I to judge?*

Two hours passed while the members of Oppo Three ate, sat through a briefing, and tweaked their gear. Then they boarded the helo and it took off.

Captain Gates was in charge of the base's command center, which was staffed by Americans and Hondurans, all seated in front of screens.

Gates, or "Gizmo" as some people called him, saw Brody but didn't acknowledge him. And that was understandable because after his return to base, Brody had taken the intel officer aside for a private conversation, the essence of which was that Gates was on thin ice.

"Cutting us off while we were in a dangerous situation was unacceptable," Brody told him. "What the fuck were you thinking?"

"There was a whole lot of shit going on," Gates said defensively. "I had to choose. And, at that particular moment, you weren't under fire."

"Well, I have to choose as well," Brody told him. "I have to choose whether I'm going to kick your ass or not. So, if you want to stay out of the hospital, I suggest that you do your fucking job. Capeesh?"

Rather than usher Brody and Medina into the adjoining conference room himself, Gates sent a sergeant to do the job, while pretending to be busy.

Brody and Medina sat on opposite sides of a table as they looked up at a flat screen TV. It displayed what the Gray Eagle drone "saw," and that was very little at the moment.

Street lights glowed in the distance, headlights passed,

and the moon was up. And that was fine except for one thing: There was no sign of the guards Brody expected to see on the warehouse's dimly lit roof. They'd been partially visible during daylight hours. So where were they? Perhaps it was silly to expect military style discipline from a street gang. But, with so much at stake, the sloppiness was surprising.

"I know that place," Medina said. "A man named Salazar runs it. We would close it down if it wasn't for the street wars. They consume our resources, and make it difficult to move around."

Having been in San Salvador, and seen how desperate the situation was firsthand, Brody was sympathetic. The city was a full-on shit show.

But the fact that at least half of El Salvador's cops were on the take didn't help. Gates spoke over the PA system. "Okay, the team is about two minutes out… Standby."

All eyes were on the big monitor. Nothing changed at first. Then the helo appeared, circled the warehouse, and prepared to land. Brody was worried by then. Where were the guards? Why weren't they firing at the Black Hawk?

Something was wrong. And, had Brody been in command, he would have aborted the mission. But Brody wasn't in charge, Andre was, and the helicopter landed.

Each member of Oppo Three had a helmet-mounted camera. That meant the people in the command center could watch six live feeds plus the video from the Gray Eagle drone. A tech named Matt was cutting back and forth between them which meant that the spectators saw one image at a time.

Brody held his breath as Andre approached the closet-sized structure that gave access to the stairs. Surely Salazar and his men would defend *that*.

But, as Andre started down the stairs, there was no sign of resistance. Then, when the Oppo leader's headlamp found a dead body at the foot of the stairway, the truth became evident. A fight *had* taken place. And Salazar's *Tigres* had lost.

The extent of that loss became more and more apparent as the Oppo Three operators spread out. Beams of light crisscrossed each other. More bodies were discovered. Three of which had their hands tied behind them and had clearly been executed.

At that point Brody was wondering about Hayden. Had the vice president been killed? Or abducted yet again?

Gates was wondering the same thing. "Five… This is Seven. Search every nook and cranny of that place. Over."

"On it," Andre replied. "Nothing so far. Over."

Minutes passed. Then, Andre spoke again. His headlamp was focused on an empty bed, a side table with medical supplies on it, and some castoff clothing. "Seven, this is Five. I think Chicago was held here. Then a second group raided the warehouse, and took him away. Over."

Brody agreed. But *how?*

The question went unanswered as Oppo Three prepared to exfil. One by one they climbed the stairs and arrived on the roof. The helo was still there, rotors turning, until it wasn't.

There was a bright flash of light, followed by a *BOOM*, and the Oppo feeds snapped to black. That left just one for Matt to use. The one from the drone circling overhead.

The force of the blast lifted the helicopter up off the roof, where it seemed to hang suspended for a moment, before diving into the raging inferno inside the warehouse.

Gouts of flame shot out through windows, a wall crumbled, and an avalanche of fiery debris flowed down onto a street. Medina said, "Holy Mother of God," and crossed himself.

Brody said, "God damn it to hell! It was a trap!"

It was obvious that someone, long gone by now, had been present to trigger the explosives. From a neighboring roof most likely. *Why?* For propaganda purposes? Something like that.

What mattered was the fact that Hayden's life was still in danger, and he'd been abducted once again. By whom? And where were they?

Possibilities were stuttering through Brody's mind as he returned to the command center. "Matt! Replay the drone footage starting at the point when Lieutenant Perez and I left the area. Let's see who entered the warehouse, and when they did so."

Matt turned to Gates who nodded. So, Matt went to work, and it wasn't long before the footage was ready. That was when the long, tedious process of watching hours of footage began.

They tried to use fast forward, but soon discovered that doing so made it impossible to assign identifiers to the pedestrians who came and went from the building.

And there were vehicles too, which entered via the downward sloping drive on the southside, and eventually left again. They included gun trucks, two box trucks, and occasional motorcycles.

Once the review was complete Brody took a moment to review his notes. There was a good deal of gibberish. But there, in capital letters, were the words "BOX TRUCKS!"

Why were they important? Because they entered and left the warehouse, yes. But more than that, there was writing on the trucks. Logos perhaps? And if so, what did they say?

The drone's camera had been too far away for Brody to read the words without magnification. Matt was preparing to leave and Brody stopped him. "Two white trucks were visible on the drone footage. They arrived and departed together. Can you bring them up please?"

Matt returned to his chair. It took the better part of ten minutes to find the trucks, freeze one of them, and increase the size of the image. "*Alquiler de camiones Florez.*"

"That translates to Florez Rental Trucks," the tech told him.

Brody looked around. Inspector Medina was talking to Colonel Patterson, who was visibly depressed. Brody hurried to join them. "I'm sorry to interrupt sir, but I need the Inspector's help."

"Of course," Medina said. "What can I do?"

"Two trucks, both of which had Florez company logos, entered and left the warehouse," Brody told him. "Taken together, they could have been used to transport men and explosives. Why Salazar's gang allowed them to enter I don't know. Some sort of scam probably."

Patterson frowned. "So, you think the Florez company is involved?"

"Maybe," Brody answered. "But, since Florez is a rental company, it's possible that the attackers rented the trucks. It's my hope that the Inspector can call the company and get the information we need."

Medina agreed to try. However, due to the late hour, most of the Florez company's employees had gone home, and the night watchman was reluctant to call them at first.

But finally, after increasingly dire threats from Medina, the watchman acquiesced and called the owner. Señor Florez was cranky at first, but became more cooperative once he learned that Medina was a police inspector. However, in order to identify the person, or persons, who rented the vehicle, Florez had to drive to the office and examine the company's records.

So, the better part of an hour dragged by before Florez called in. Patterson put the call on speakerphone. "I have it!" the business man announced. "The credit card they used belongs to the Red Dawn Shipping Company."

Gates was there, and turned to a tech. "Quick! Go online and search for the Red Dawn Shipping Company."

WILLIAM C. DIETZ

Keys *clicked* as the tech typed. "Got it, sir …. Take a look."

The tech exited her chair so the others could see. There was an introduction, accompanied by a photo of a ship, and a description. All of them skimmed it. Patterson was the first to finish. "Shit, shit, shit. The company is headquartered in Venezuela!"

All of them knew what that meant. Venezuela was aligned with the Axis. Not formally, but aligned nevertheless.

Brody turned to Patterson. "I think we need help, sir. Maybe the CIA is familiar with the Red Dawn Shipping Company. And maybe the National Reconnaissance people can spot the ship we're looking for. It's probably at sea by now …. But it shouldn't be that far away."

Patterson produced a jerky nod. "Let's find out."

The White House, Washington D.C.

President Dearing was in bed, asleep, when the phone next to her bed rang. As always, she attempted to take the call by the third ring in order to spare her husband. She failed. He grumbled and rolled over. "Yes?"

"I'm sorry to disturb you, Madam President," Secretary of State Boyko said. "But you asked me to call."

"Is this about the raid in El Salvador?"

"Yes."

"It failed."

"Yes."

Dearing swung her feet over and onto the floor. "How bad was it?"

"All six members of Oppo Three were killed in an explosion."

Dearing was silent as she wiped the tears away. It wasn't the first time, and the president managed to keep her voice level. "I'm sorry to hear that."

"It gets worse," Boyko said.

"How so?"

"We have reason to believe that the vice president is aboard a Venezuelan cargo ship already at sea."

"Options?"

"There are no tier one SMUs (Special Missions Units) nearby. The nearest force we have is Joint Task Force-Bravo, which is stationed at Soto Cano Air Base in Honduras. And the commanding officer, a colonel named Patterson, is requesting permission to carry out an airborne VBSS."

Dearing knew that the letters VBSS stood for "Visit, board, search and seizure."

Had the request been for a VBSS on an Alliance vessel, Dearing would have been in a bind. The U.S. couldn't afford to lose strategic partners.

But Venezuela had formerly aligned itself with the Axis, even if it wasn't sending troops, so fuck them. Come to think of it, Dearing reasoned, the Venezuelans could have conceived the secondary operation themselves.

Or, had they been directed to snatch Hayden by Russia or China? Either one of which would love to capture the American and use him for propaganda purposes.

Dearing made a mental note to have the CIA look into all of the possibilities. "A VBSS is approved," Dearing said. "And Andy?"

"Ma'am?"

"Tell the men and women of Task Force-Bravo that I said, 'Thank you.'"

Over the Pacific Ocean, West of El Salvador

After some frantic research at the NRO (National Reconnaissance Office) and the CIA, it was determined that Vice President Hayen was probably aboard the *Southern Cross,* a vessel owned by Red Dawn Shipping, which had departed El Salvador bound for Panama.

And that was why four helicopters, including two Apache gunships and two Black Hawks, were racing out to sea.

Brody's team was aboard the first Black Hawk, designated Thunder-One, while Perez and her soldiers were flying on Thunder-Two.

A Honduran naval officer named Vegas, and two of his sailors, were on Thunder-One with Brody.

The plan was deceptively simple. Assuming everything went well, the AH-64 Apaches would force the ship to heave to, allowing soldiers to fast rope down onto the vessel's main deck, where they were to eliminate resistance if any.

Then, after seizing control of the vessel, the team would search for Vice President Hayden and free him. It was simple. One, two, and three.

So why was Brody scared? Because he could fail, because he could get killed, and because he could lose Perez. That would rip him apart. How was such a thing possible? To develop such feelings in a matter of days. It didn't matter. What was, was.

Brody's reverie came to an abrupt end as the pilot spoke over the intercom. "We have visual contact with the vessel."

Brody was wearing a headset and could communicate with all four helicopter pilots at once, or individually. "This is Skyhook-Six. All aircraft will circle the ship while Sea-Dog attempts to make contact. Over."

Brody heard a series of mike clicks by way of a response. Vegas, AKA "Sea-Dog," was crouched by the open door and speaking into a handheld VHF radio as the slipstream tore at his clothing. English was the world's official maritime language.

"*Southern Cross*, this is Joint Task Force-Bravo, operating in conjunction with the U.S., Honduran, and El Salvadoran governments. You are hereby ordered to reduce speed and heave to. Please confirm."

By that time Brody was standing behind the officer, looking out over his head. The *Southern Cross* was a general cargo ship with deck cranes forward and a three-story superstructure aft. Spray flew away from her bow as the ship broke through the oncoming waves.

Vegas looked back over his shoulder. "They're ignoring us, sir."

Brody swore. "Warhorse-One, this is Skyhook-Six. Fire across the ship's bow. Over."

The reply was a laconic, "Roger that," as an Apache gunship broke away, came in low, and fired its 30mm M230E1 Chain Gun. It was a short burst. But the geysers were clear to see. And Brody expected the freighter to slow down.

But it didn't. Brody saw a spark of light, followed by a puff of smoke, as a member of the ship's crew fired a shoulder launched missile at Warhorse-Two.

However, thanks to the DIRCM (Directional Infrared Countermeasures) system on the Apache, the missile turned away and exploded over the sea.

Brody faced some difficult choices. He could try to land his teams without compliance. But that would involve hovering over the ship so low that the enemy weapons couldn't miss.

Or, he could order one of the gunships to attack. But what if Vice President Hayden were killed? And, where was the VP anyway? Locked up in the superstructure? Or confined below deck?

Brody decided to assume the latter. "Warhorse-Two, this is Skyhook... Put a couple of rockets into the ship's superstructure. But stay off of the bridge. That's where the controls are."

Brody was aboard "Thunder-One," and thanks to the pilot, the helicopter was positioned to provide him with a good view of what happened next. Warhorse-Two decided to approach the *Southern Cross* low and attack bow-on.

Hydra launchers were hanging under the Apache's pylons, and Brody saw flashes as the rockets took off, and watched them go in.

The Hydras weren't radar-guided, like the larger Hellfire missiles were, which meant that a good deal of skill was required to hit anything. But the superstructure was a big target. So, there was reason to be hopeful. Assuming at least one of the rockets struck home, there was a good chance that the Venezuelans would surrender.

Then Brody heard Warhorse-Two swear, saw the rockets hit the windows that fronted the bridge, and explode in unison. Flames appeared, smoke poured out of the wound, and the freighter lurched to port. Brody figured the wheel was gone, along with the helmsman, and whoever was standing nearby. The captain? Maybe. It didn't matter. The ship was out of control.

✪

Vice President Hayden was lying on what had been the third mate's bunk. It was located in a cabin so small that there wasn't room for anything other than a metal locker, a toilet and the bunk.

Something was wrong. It didn't take a genius to figure that out. The ship was rolling from side to side, and Hayden could hear gunfire. There were two possibilities: A rescue or another snatch. Meaning still *another* group attempting to seize control of him.

Hayden figured that the first possibility was the more likely of the two and was determined to help. The problem was that he was tired, very tired, and felt dizzy whenever he tried to stand. Yet that was precisely what he needed to do.

But first, Hayden had to retrieve his secret weapon, which was a four-tined dinner fork. He'd acquired it the previous day by hiding the tool in the crevice between his mattress and the bulkhead during a faked coughing fit. An incident that seemed to be so serious that the guard forgot to inventory the silverware.

Hayden felt for it, wrapped his fingers around cold metal, and brought the weapon out. Then, by an act of will, he managed to swing his bare feet off the bed and onto the cold deck. Hayden's center of balance shifted as the freighter rolled, causing him to grab hold of the locker, or risk a fall.

Then it was time for Hayden to take his place in the corner where, when someone opened the hatch, he wouldn't be seen. The ship lurched, Hayden battled to remain upright and closed his eyes. His wife Elaine was there waiting for him with a smile on her face. Hayden began to cry.

"Sorry Skyhook," the pilot said, as his rockets hit the bridge. "My bad. Over."

"This is Skyhook," Brody said. "Thunders One and Two will drop their teams as planned. We can do this. Over."

Brody turned to the team of hand-picked soldiers. "Prepare to fast rope. Prepare to fight. Any questions?"

"Yes, sir," a private said. "Is it too late to visit the shitter?"

"That's what your pants are for," Sergeant Belko replied. "Let's do this thing."

The process was relatively simple. A thick rope, typically about two-inches in diameter, was dropped from a helicopter. Then, using heat-resistant gloves to protect their hands, the soldiers would slide down the line like beads on a string.

After touching down, each soldier would exit the landing zone, shed his or her gloves, and prepare to fire. All in a matter of minutes.

"We're taking fire!" the helo's door gunner shouted, as he fired at the deck below. Shiny casings flew, fell, and *rattled* around the deck.

Brody had assigned himself to the one slot. He stepped

up to the rope and saw that the ship was broadside to the waves. She was rocking from side to side and taking blow after blow. A sure sign that there was no one at the helm. A bullet snapped past Brody's head.

He made a grab for the rope, swung out, and felt gravity take over. The ship rolled alarmingly, and bullets sparked the deck in front of Brody as he landed.

The enemy marksman was high up, in the cab of a deck crane, with a good view of the entire deck. His head and shoulders were visible but nothing else.

Brody's XM7 rifle was equipped with a Close Combat Optic system. The crosshairs seemed to float onto the cab, the trigger gave, and a burst of 6.8mm passed through sheet metal and kept on going. The sniper disappeared from sight.

Vegas appeared next to him. "We need to bring the ship under control, sir. The emergency steering controls are probably located below deck in the stern. With your permission I'll head down there and try to regain control."

Brody was grateful for the guidance. "Go for it. And take your sailors with you. Who knows what you'll run into. I'll try to reach the bridge."

Vegas nodded. "Yes, sir." As the Honduran and his men made their way aft, along the starboard side of the ship, a machine gun *rattled* and bullets splattered around them. But none were hit and they disappeared from sight.

Brody, Perez, and most of their soldiers were still in the bow, gathered around the ship's capstan—a winch used for a variety of tasks including loading or unloading cargo. In order to reach the ship's superstructure, Brody's team would have to cross a lot of open deck and expose themselves to gunfire from crew members hidden behind some of the deck cargo.

But, if Brody's idea worked, the standoff was about to end. "Warhorse-One and Warhorse-Two…this is Skyhook-Six. We're pinned down in the bow of the ship. The hostiles are on the port side hiding behind a stack of shipping containers. Give them a strong dose of thirty mike-mike. Over."

"We'll try," Warhorse-One replied. "Then Warhorse-Two and I will have to haul ass. We're bingo fuel. Over."

"Roger that," Brody replied. "Over."

Brody was hopeful. But the memory of the way the rocket had destroyed the bridge was fresh in his mind, so he knew success was anything but certain.

The soldiers watched as the Apaches *roared* in and opened fire. The nearly simultaneous attacks lasted no more than a couple of seconds each, but were sufficient to chew large holes in the cargo containers, and slaughter those using them for cover. Brody stood and shouted. "Follow me!" And his soldiers did. Not a shot was fired as they crossed the deck.

Bodies, and parts of bodies, were strewn about. But in spite of the horror, one thing was obvious. And Perez gave voice to it. "What the hell? These people are Asian."

Brody took it in. Chinese? Of course. That made perfect sense.

✪

The sound of helicopters roaring overhead was so loud that Hayden didn't realize the hatch had been opened until cold metal came into contact with his chest. He waited for the soldier to move forward, stepped in behind him, and attacked. The fork came in at an angle, the tines went deep, and blood spurted.

The soldier tried to turn. But it was too late. And, as the fork stabbed in and out, both men screamed. Warm blood spurted onto Hayden's hand as he clutched his victim's coat. *Don't faint .... Don't faint .... Don't faint.*

Their eyes met. Hayden saw the light fade from the

young man's eyes and knew the soldier was dead. He released his grip and heard a soft *thump* as the body landed on the deck.

Hayden stood there, body swaying, as he struggled to remain vertical. But as the ship rolled, he lost consciousness. The dead man cushioned his fall. Darkness took him in.

✪

Perez and her soldiers were searching for Hayden. Brody was on the fire blackened bridge. Cold air surged in through the shattered windows, the controls had been destroyed, and three bodies lay on the deck. An intermittent buzzing sound was heard. A soldier grabbed the handset labeled "Engine Room," and listened. Then he waved to Brody. "It's Lieutenant Vegas, sir."

Brody went over to take the phone. "This is Brody."

"I found the emergency controls," Vegas said. "And we're turning back. A tug has been dispatched and should meet us in roughly two hours."

"Good work," Brody said. "I'll post a soldier on this phone in case you need anything."

No sooner had Brody replaced the phone, than his radio burped static, and the call he'd been waiting for came in. It was from Perez. "Skyhook-Six, this is Five. We found Chicago. But he's in bad shape. We need an air evac. Over."

"This is Thunder-One," a male voice said. "We're low on fuel, and about to head back. But Wombat-One and Two are five out. Two has a doctor onboard. Over."

"Thanks for everything," Brody replied. "We'll get ready. Over."

One of the ship's basket stretchers was used to transport Hayden to the bow while Wombat-Two dropped a cable. The ship was bow on to the waves by that time, so the rolling had been replaced by a back-and-forth pitching motion, which was almost as bad.

Tons of water came over the bow, landed on the deck,

and threatened to carry Hayden away. Brody threw himself across the vice president's legs, and managed to hold the stretcher in place, as soldiers hooked the dangling cable to the waiting harness.

Brody stood and thumbed his radio. "Chicago is ready! Pull him up!"

Rain splattered on Brody's face as he looked up. The helicopter's nav lights were on, and it was swaying as the pilot battled to hold the aircraft steady. The stretcher rose in a series of jerks, steadied a bit, and continued to rise.

Finally, after what seemed like an eternity, the vice president reached the point where the Black Hawk's crew could pull him in. Once Hayden was aboard, the Black Hawk turned toward land and sped away. Brody felt a tremendous sense of relief as the helo vanished to the east.

But there was still work to do. Three prisoners were under lock and key, all in separate compartments, and had to be guarded.

There were documents too. Most of which were in what Brody assumed was Chinese, all of which had to be photographed where they'd been found, prior to being boxed. And there were laptops. Three of them. Which would definitely be of interest to various security organizations.

Then, as the ship continued to pitch forward and back, nearly two dozen bodies had to be searched and photographed. Finally, after the tug arrived and took the *Red Dawn* under tow, helicopters went to work pulling the Americans up off the ship.

Perez and her soldiers had orders to remain aboard. Brody didn't like that, but had no say in the matter, and continued to worry about her during the flight to the Soto Cano Airbase.

Once on the ground Brody had trouble standing. It felt as though he was still on the ship, which was pitching forward and back, as he staggered away from the Black Hawk.

But that didn't stop Captain Gates, and two recently arrived CIA agents, from putting him through a so-called "hotwash," to ensure that every dribble of information he could provide was properly recorded, annotated, and stored.

That included the recon mission, the fight with the Barrio 6 gang, and the rescue at sea. All of it. A process that Gates clearly relished.

Then, and only then, was Brody allowed to leave the headquarters building, and return to his quarters. At last, it was time to pee, collapse on the bed fully clothed, and enter sleep's welcome embrace.

Brody didn't arise until noon the following day. When he tried to call Perez, he ran into voicemail. "I'm on detached duty. Please leave a message."

Brody left a message asking Perez to call, but she didn't, which suggested she was still aboard the *Red Dawn*.

Meanwhile, according to what Brody had heard, Vice President Hayden's condition was improving. And those who'd been wounded during the mission were on the mend as well.

After working his way through a pile of paperwork, and eating a solitary dinner, Brody hit the rack. He awoke feeling rested, and was just about to shower, when there was a knock on the door. Dressed in nothing more than pajama bottoms, Brody went to answer it.

And there, rather than the messenger Brody expected, was Marie Perez. She was dressed in civies. "Good morning! I like the view."

"You're back," Brody said. "I tried to reach you."

"I was busy," Perez replied. "Now go inside, shower, and pack a bag. I managed to arrange for some leave. Separately, of course. Unless you don't want to go."

Brody's eyebrows rose. "That's awesome! Where are we going?"

"To Costa Rico," Perez answered.

"A good choice. Please come in."

"I can't," Perez said. "It wouldn't look right. Tio Alberto is parked just outside the main gate. Meet me there."

"I certainly will," Brody replied, and watched her walk away. Perez was a lot of things, but shy wasn't one of them. And Brody liked that.

Brody hurried to shave, shower, and pack. It was a short hike to the gate. Two of his soldiers were on duty. Both wore huge grins as they saluted. "Watch your six, sir," one of them said. "El Salvador is a dangerous place."

Brody grinned. "You guys would know."

Thanks to Tio Alberto's rep and largesse they made it to the airport in record time. Brody tried to pay but Alberto refused. "Family members travel for free, Captain Jim. Don't worry, I won't tell Camila."

Their plane departed on time, and the flight was just long enough for them to have a drink and catch up. The landing at San Jose International Airport was smooth, their luggage arrived quickly, and a rental car was waiting. Perez was nothing if not efficient.

The drive to the seaside resort of Jaco was supposed to take an hour and a half, but they arrived fifteen minutes earlier than that, because Perez had a lead foot. Bit by bit, Brody was learning more about the woman sitting next to him. And the process was delightful.

Once the ride was over, they checked into what turned out to be a very nice room. Then, after changing clothes, they went straight to the beach.

Striped tents were available for a price, which Brody happily paid for one, both for the additional shade and some privacy. They were inside, preparing for a swim, when Perez dropped her wrap.

Brody was transfixed. He knew Perez was pretty, and shapely as well. But he'd never seen her in a white bikini. And she was, to put it mildly, stunning.

Perez put one hand on a hip and smiled. "So, Captain …. Will I pass inspection?"

Brody took her into his arms. She looked up at him, eyes closed, ready for a kiss.

One thing led to another, pleasure was given, and pleasure was taken. And as they lay side by side, Brody looked into her eyes. "I will never forget this moment. Thank you."

Perez smiled. "It was Abuela Camila's idea. 'A vacation,' That's what she said. 'Your mother went away with your father, and that's how Maria One came to be.' Do you remember when she touched your face?" Perez demanded. "'This is the one.' That's what she said. And my Abuela is always right."

Brody kissed her. And Perez kissed him back.

The sun sank towards the horizon. Waves slid up over the sand. And, many miles to the north, a blind woman smiled.

AUTHOR'S NOTES

FOR those who keep track of such things a focused laser, like the one used in this story, could theoretically be used to target a specific location on Earth from orbit. But, for now, limitations in technology mean that precise targeting is still out of reach and would be made even more difficult if the goal was to hit a plane in flight.

The problems include the Earth's atmosphere, which could distort a laser beam, limiting its effectiveness especially from long distances.

But as huge corporations vie with each other to develop space tourism, lunar landers, and missions to Mars—it seems likely that the technologies required for orbital energy weapons will be spun off and inevitably used. I hope I'm wrong.

www.ingramcontent.com/pod-product-compliance
Lightning Source LLC
Chambersburg PA
CBHW022053170626
46808CB00003B/1454